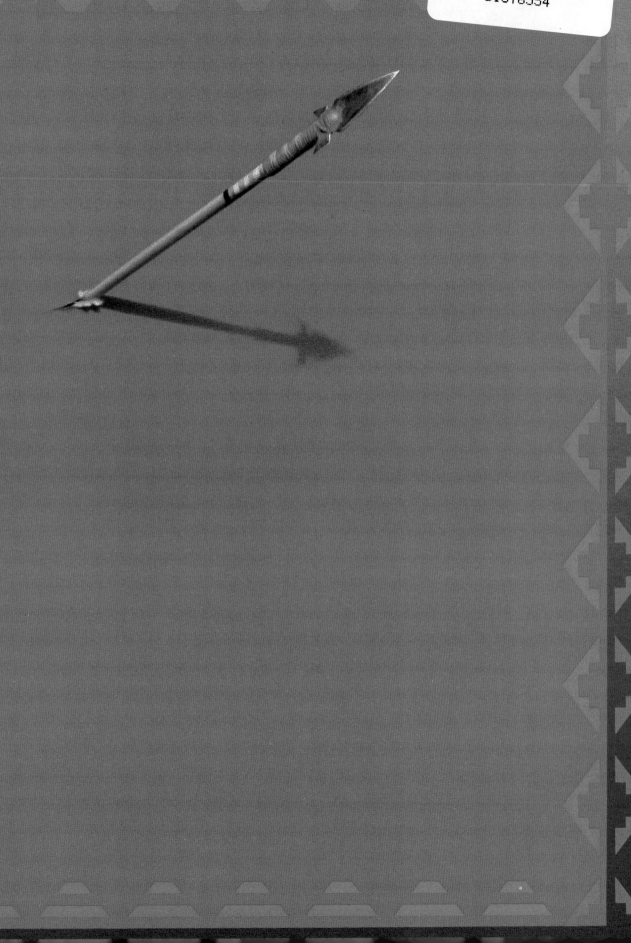

EDITOR'S NOTE

This story is adapted from a tale included in volume 1 of a collection by Ruth Benedict titled *Zuni Mythology,* which was published in 1935 by Columbia University Press. There are numerous versions of this tale, though all share the theme of youth slaying a monster. In the introduction to her collection, Benedict explains that in Zuni mythology many variations of a folktale coexist, making it impossible to designate one version as *the* tribal tale. She points out that variations in a tale result from combinations of incidents in different plot sequences and do not necessarily reflect historical differences or the interpretations of specific storytellers.

Requests for permission to make copies of any part of the work should be mailed to:
Permissions Department, Harcourt Brace & Company, 6277 Sea Harbor Drive, Orlando, Florida 32887-6777.

This is a translation of *Ahajute und der Wolkenfresser.*
First U.S. edition 1996

Library of Congress Cataloging-in-Publication Data
Hulpach, Vladimir.
Ahaiyute and Cloud Eater / written by Vladimir Hulpach;
illustrated by Marek Zawadzki.
p. cm.
Summary: A retelling of a Zuni folktale in which an Indian boy accepts the challenge to
conquer Cloud Eater and thereby prove that he is a strong warrior.
ISBN 0-15-201237-0
1. Zuni Indians—Folklore. 2. Legends—New Mexico. [1. Zuni Indians—Folklore.
2. Indians of North America—New Mexico—Folklore. 3. Folklore—New Mexico.]
I. Zawadzki, Marek, ill. II. Title.
E99.Z9H85 1996
398.2'089979—dc20
[E] 95-40911

The text was set in Meridien.

A B C D E

Printed in Turnhout, Belgium

AHAIYUTE
AND CLOUD EATER

VLADIMIR HULPACH

ILLUSTRATED BY
Marek Zawadzki

HARCOURT BRACE & COMPANY
San Diego   New York   London

Far from all the oceans,
in a land where the sun
baked the ground hard,
there rose a mountain
that towered above the clouds.
From a distance, it looked like a
corncob, and so it was called
Corn Mountain.

Ahaiyute lived with his
grandmother at the top of
Corn Mountain.
The time had come for him to
accomplish a great deed to prove
himself a strong warrior.

Ahaiyute was as nimble as
an antelope, as sleek as a
trout, and as strong as a
buffalo. He needed only to
find a worthy challenge.
Time passed, and his
friends proved themselves
warriors and became men.
But Ahaiyute still waited
for his time. He became
restless and hardly
touched the food that
Grandmother prepared.

One day Grandmother
called Ahaiyute to her.
He bent close to hear her soft
voice. "There is a monster that
has settled in the East,"
she said. "But I warn you,
he is dangerous."

"He is as big as Corn Mountain," Grandmother continued.
"And when he opens his mouth, it reaches
from one end of the horizon to the other."
She stretched her arms wide. "He lives by eating clouds,
and that is why it hardly ever rains
and people and animals die of thirst."

"And no one has been found who can conquer Cloud Eater?" Ahaiyute asked.

Grandmother shook her head, her silver braids brushing her shoulders. "Many have tried. None have ever returned."

"I will return," Ahaiyute promised.

"The fight will not be equal," Grandmother said.
"To help you, I will give you four magic feathers."

"If you put the red feather in your hair," Grandmother continued, "it will lead you to Cloud Eater. The blue feather will give you the power to speak the language of the animals. The yellow feather will make you small enough to fit into a mousehole. And the black feather will give you great strength."

Ahaiyute packed the four magic feathers with great care, and before the birds had stopped singing for the evening, he stood before Grandmother, ready for his journey. He said good-bye, put the red feather in his hair, and left Corn Mountain far behind.

His journey took him
farther and farther east, until he reached the land of
Cloud Eater. The earth was hard and cracked, the grass
was as brittle as tinder. All life seemed
to have withered and died. The only creature in
sight was a little mole that peered curiously at
the wanderer from its pueblo.

Ahaiyute placed the blue feather in his hair.

"Do you know where Cloud Eater lives?" he asked Mole.

"He lives a few sunrises from here," Mole answered.
"But you must not let him see you. Look around you.
He has destroyed every living thing near and far.
He cannot harm me because I live underground."

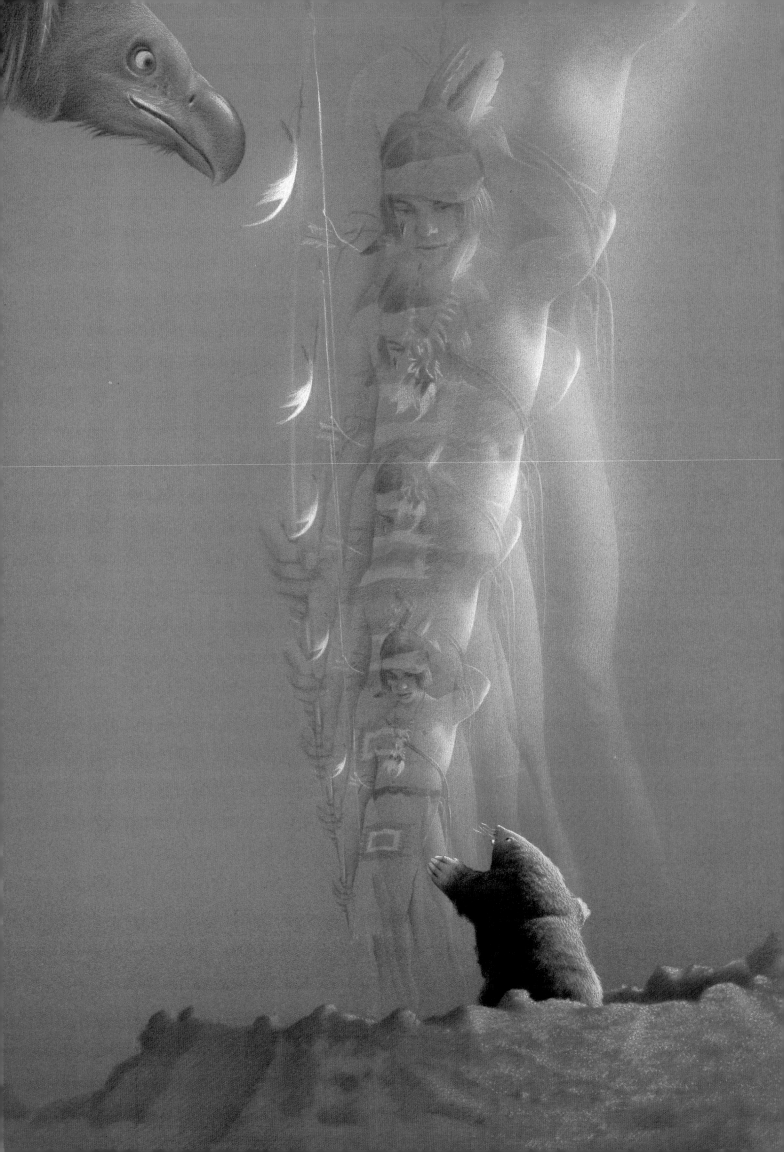

Remembering the third feather, Ahaiyute put it in his hair. He shrank until he was the size of Mole. Now Ahaiyute could fit through Mole's tunnel. He would be safe from Cloud Eater.

"Will you show me the way to Cloud Eater?" Ahaiyute asked.

"I would be honored to show you," Mole replied. "Not only are you brave but you are clever. None who came before you asked me for help. Maybe if they had, they would not have died. Follow me."

Even though Ahaiyute was now
small, he had to bend down to fit
through the passage.
He stumbled unsteadily
after Mole, his eyes not
used to the dark.

Mole and Ahaiyute stopped
now and then to rest and eat.
Mole had stored food and water
in the tunnels.

They continued on their journey,
and the path began to wind
and turn back on itself.

"Now we are under
Cloud Eater's pueblo," Mole said.
"Feel the earth tremble."

A few large stones crashed
down into the passage
and the walls shook.

Mole said quietly, "Cloud Eater is
tossing and turning in his sleep.
We have a little farther to go."

The tunnel widened and
led into a large room.
The ceiling rose and fell
with the monster's snoring.

Dull beats could be heard
from above. "That is
Cloud Eater's heartbeat," Mole
whispered. "You will have to be
very strong for your arrow to
reach him through the earth."

Ahaiyute heard
Cloud Eater's terrible snoring,
and he reached for the last
feather. Placing the black feather
in his hair, he planted his feet
firmly and reached in his quiver
for the arrow with the sharpest
tip. Ahaiyute fitted it to his
bowstring and aimed at the point
where the ceiling dropped lowest
toward the ground.

Ahaiyute drew back his
bowstring as far as he could, took
a deep breath, and released the
arrow. It sailed straight through
the air and disappeared into the
dirt. The ceiling began to
crumble, and Ahaiyute's ears felt
ready to burst as Cloud Eater
began to wail. The earth beneath
Ahaiyute rose and fell as if
shaken by an earthquake, and he
tried to steady himself. Dust
clouded the air. Peering through
the darkness, he thought
he saw light from outside.
He rushed toward it.
At once he was knocked flat to
the ground, and his mouth was
filled with dirt as the ceiling
collapsed around him.

Ahaiyute's head pounded.
He slowly opened his eyes.
To his surprise, he was lying in
the grass—not buried beneath the
earth. Mole wiped his forehead
with a damp cloth and patted his
cheeks. Ahaiyute gently shook his
head from side to side, then sat up.

"Did I kill Cloud Eater?"
Ahaiyute asked.

"See for yourself." Mole pointed to
the lifeless, snakelike body of
Cloud Eater. "It was magnificent!"
Mole rejoiced. "Your arrow struck
him through the heart. As he died,
Cloud Eater thrashed and flailed
and buried you with stones and
earth. But I dug a new passage and
pulled you out. Ahaiyute, you
have done a great thing today."

Ahaiyute lay back on the ground,
exhausted. He looked up at the sky,
where low-hanging rain clouds
were already beginning
to form. They would bring
water to his country
and signal to his people that
Ahaiyute had become a man.